Nate the Great

and the
Wandering
Word

Nate the Great

and the
Wandering
Word

by Marjorie Weinman Sharmat
and Andrew Sharmat

illustrated by Jody Wheeler
in the style of Marc Simont

A YEARLING BOOK

ACKNOWLEDGMENTS

Jody Wheeler would like to thank Nancy Chambers
and her greenwing macaw, Mojo, the model for Pip's parrot.

Text copyright © 2018 by Marjorie Weinman Sharmat and Andrew Sharmat
Cover art and interior illustrations copyright © 2018 by Jody Wheeler
Extra Fun Activities copyright © 2019 by Emily Costello
Extra Fun Activities illustrations copyright © 2019 by Jody Wheeler

All rights reserved. Published in the United States by Yearling, an imprint of
Random House Children's Books, a division of Penguin Random House LLC,
New York. Originally published in hardcover in the United States by Delacorte Press,
an imprint of Random House Children's Books, New York, in 2018.

New illustrations of Nate the Great, Sludge, Rosamond, Annie, Claude, Harry, Fang,
and the Hexes by Jody Wheeler based upon original drawings by Marc Simont.

Yearling and the jumping horse design are registered trademarks of Penguin Random House LLC.

Visit us on the Web! rhcbooks.com

Educators and librarians, for a variety of teaching tools, visit us at RHTeachersLibrarians.com

The Library of Congress has cataloged the hardcover edition of this work as follows:
Names: Sharmat, Marjorie Weinman, author. | Sharmat, Andrew, author. | Wheeler, Jody, illustrator.
Title: Nate the Great and the wandering word / by Marjorie Weinman Sharmat
and Andrew Sharmat ; illustrated by Jody Wheeler in the style of Marc Simont.
Description: First edition. | New York : Delacorte Press, [2018] |
Summary: "Nate the Great helps his friend Esmeralda find the word she wrote down that was going
to be the name of the upcoming pet concert, before it's too late"— Provided by publisher.
Identifiers: LCCN 2017038518 (print) | LCCN 2017050294 (ebook) |
ISBN 978-1-5247-6546-0 (el) | ISBN 978-1-5247-6544-6 (hc) | ISBN 978-1-5247-6545-3 (glb)
Subjects: | CYAC: Mystery and detective stories. | Lost and found possessions—Fiction. |
BISAC: JUVENILE FICTION / Readers / Chapter Books. | JUVENILE FICTION / Social Issues / Friendship.
Classification: LCC PZ7.S5299 (ebook) | LCC PZ7.S5299 Navl 2018 (print) |
DDC [Fic]—dc23

ISBN 978-1-5247-6547-7 (pbk.)

Printed in the United States of America
10 9 8 7 6 5 4 3
First Yearling Edition 2019

Chapter One
Questions and Answers

 M y name is Nate the Great.

I am a detective.

My partner is my dog, Sludge.

One morning we were out for a walk.

Suddenly, someone called to us.

It was Esmeralda.

Esmeralda is very smart.

She knows many things.

"Hey, Nate. Hey, Sludge," she called.

"I have lost something."

I was surprised.

"What did you lose?" I asked.

"I lost a word," Esmeralda said.

"What?" I said. "How did you lose a word?"

Esmeralda sighed. "Well, I had it
and then I didn't," she said.

I was interested. Sludge looked
interested too.

"Hmm," I said. "Did you write the word
or just say it?"

"I said it *and* wrote it on pink paper.
Now I don't remember the word.
Please find it for me."

"I, Nate the Great, will take the case,"
I said.

"I will look for your word.
First, I have questions to ask you.

WHEN did you lose the word?
WHERE did you lose the word?
HOW did you lose the word?"
"I have answers to your questions,"
Esmeralda said.
"I lost my word yesterday.
I was at Rosamond's house.
I was at her dining room table. It was noon.
I wrote my word and then it was gone."
"Did Rosamond see you write the word
on the pink paper?" I asked.
"No, Rosamond was in the kitchen,"
Esmeralda said.

"She wants to have a pet singing concert.
She was testing pets' singing voices."
"Who else was in the house?" I asked.
"The kitchen was full of people,"
Esmeralda said. "And pets too.
Finley's rat; Oliver's eel; Claude's pig;
Annie's dog, Fang; and Rosamond's four cats.
The pets were in the kitchen for tryouts."
"So you were alone in the dining room?"
I asked.

"Almost," Esmeralda said. "Pip's parrot is afraid of Rosamond's cats. He was with me."

"Smart bird," I said. "But where was Pip?"

"In the kitchen, listening to the tryouts," Esmeralda said. "Are those good clues?"

"I don't know yet," I said. "What were you writing about when your word disappeared?"

"I was trying to come up with a name for the concert. I wrote the word down so I wouldn't forget it.

"Then I remembered that I had to be home
for lunch. When I came back later,
my word was gone."
"Can you tell me anything about the word?"
I asked.

"Yes," Esmeralda said. "It's a long word. A strange word. A made-up word."

"A strange word will be right at home in Rosamond's house," I said.

"Now here comes my best clue," Esmeralda said.

"When I came back, all the pets were gone too. But Annie's little brother, Harry, was in the dining room with scissors.

"He was cutting words out of sentences.
I thought my word was mixed in
with the words he had cut, but I couldn't
find it anywhere."
I, Nate the Great, knew it was time to go
home and think.
I wrote a note to my mother.

Dear Mother —
Sludge and I are
looking for a lost word.
First we have to think.
I will eat a pancake
and think. Sludge will
eat a bone and think.
Then we have to be brave.
We must look in the
house of Rosamond
and her cats, the
Hexes. We will be back...
We hope.
Love,
Nate the great

Chapter Two
Words and Clothes

After we ate, Sludge and I went
to Rosamond's house.
Rosamond was home. So were her four cats,
Plain Hex, Little Hex, Big Hex, and
Super Hex.

Rosamond had ink on her dress.
Esmeralda was also there.
She was searching for her word.
"Hello," I said. "Sludge and I are trying
to find Esmeralda's lost word."
Rosamond smiled. "Words get lost
all the time," she said.

"It's because a word doesn't wear
any clothes. Esmeralda's word will be
hard to find."
I stared at Rosamond.
Esmeralda stared at Rosamond.
Sludge stared at Rosamond.
I, Nate the Great, now had to find
another word, a word to describe what
I had just heard.
I couldn't find one.

Rosamond asked, "How can you look
for a word if you don't even know
what the word is?"
"I, Nate the Great, say the word will
be found."
Esmeralda began to search again.
Rosamond smiled again.
"I have a present for Esmeralda,"
she whispered to me.
"Really?" I whispered back.

"Yes. I've been looking for singing pets and I found a long-neck turtle.
Lots of great singers have long necks, so he must be a great singer."
"I don't think it works that way," I said. "Did you ask Esmeralda if she even wants a pet?"
"It will be a surprise," Rosamond said.
"A surprise, yes," I said. "Maybe not a good one. Now I must look for a long, strange, made-up word on pink paper. It will be easy to find."
"No it won't," Rosamond said. "All of my papers are pink. And I have a lot of them. And lots of words."

Chapter Three
Wardrobes for Words

Esmeralda had told us that she had lost
her word in the dining room.
Sludge sniffed his way there.
I followed him.
Sludge is a wonderful sniffer detective.

I saw pink papers covered with food.
Sludge licked the papers.
He was doing great detective work.
But I, Nate the Great, didn't know if
Sludge was just hungry.
The dining room table was also covered
with papers.

Pink papers.

On each piece of paper was a single word.

I was looking for a long, strange word.

Some of the words were long.

But none of the words were strange.

What *was* strange was the way many

of the words looked.

They looked as if they were wearing clothes.

I had to ask Rosamond why.

I was not looking forward

to hearing her answer.

"Some words are exciting," she said.
"Other words are boring. And boring words
need style. I'm here to help them.
I create wardrobes for words."

"You dress up words?" I asked.

"Yes," Rosamond said. "I am very loyal
to words."

Rosamond showed me where she had set up
a table with pencils and pens.

"Welcome to my word studio," she said.
"This is where I take boring words and
give them color and style. If I think a word
would look good in a dress, I put a dress
on it. If it needs a tie, I give it a tie.
I've been working hard. Harry is my helper.
He cuts up the words. I choose the boring
ones and give them the outfits they need."
"Where is Harry now?" I asked.
"I sent him out to deliver the dressed-up
words to all my friends with singing pets,"
Rosamond said. "Words make great gifts."
"I need to find Harry," I said. "He might
have delivered the missing word to someone
by mistake."

lost

CLoE

MoNKS

Trail

BeAch

spot

Chapter Four
Long, Strange, and Made-Up

Sludge and I went to the house where
Harry, his big sister, Annie, and her
even bigger dog, Fang, live.
Annie answered the door.
Fang showed us his fangs.

"Hello," I said. "I am on a case. I'm looking for a missing word, and I'm looking for Harry. Is he home?"

"No," Annie said. "He's out delivering gifts that Rosamond made."

"Did he give you one?" I asked.

"Yes," Annie said.

Annie handed me a piece of pink paper. There was a word on the paper.

Above the word was a drawing of a bow tie.
There was a picture of a microphone under
the word.
Rosamond had done good work.
The word was "sing."
But "sing" wasn't long.
"Sing" wasn't strange.
"Sing" wasn't Esmeralda's made-up word.

Chapter Five
Into the Mud

Our next stop was Claude's house.
Harry had delivered a word to Claude.
Maybe it was Esmeralda's word.
There was a sign on the door.

Claude answered my knock.
Sludge and I went into the house.
I hoped that I would not hear oinking.
"What have you lost today?" I asked Claude.
Claude was always losing things.
"Nothing yet. But my pig was given
something piggish," Claude said. "Harry
brought me a painting of a pig on pink paper
with bite marks. They looked like they
came from Fang's fangs."

"I would like to see your pig," I said.
Claude led us out to his yard.
He pointed to a large mud pile.
In the mud pile was his pig, Anastasia.
I, Nate the Great, did not want to search
a mud pile.

"We will search with our eyes, not with our hands," I said.

"Or our paws," I added.

Sludge wagged his tail.

Sludge and I looked into the mud.

Claude's pig started oinking.

"She's practicing for the concert," Claude said.

"She oinks like a real pro," I said.

Suddenly, I saw something pink sticking out
of the mud.
It was smack in the middle.
I, Nate the Great, would have to walk
through the mud.

I took off my shoes and socks.
I put one foot into the muck.
Squiiish!
Then the other foot.
More *squiiish!*

Sludge stayed back.
Detective work can be messy.
I reached over and grabbed the paper.
It was partly covered in mud,
but I could read the word.
"'ZooRevue.'"
I had found Esmeralda's missing word!

It was a long word. A strange word.
A made-up word.
And it sounded like the name of
Rosamond's concert.
I cleaned my feet.
Sludge and I had somewhere to go.

Chapter Six
The Quiet Pet

Sludge and I ran back to
Rosamond's house.
Our case was solved.
Sludge was wagging his tail.
If I had a tail, I would have wagged it too.
"Esmeralda," I called. "Sludge and I
found your word!"

"Clues did it!" Esmeralda shouted.
"I love clues more than ever."
I, Nate the Great, now knew that
Esmeralda thought she was a detective.
Sludge and I went inside Rosamond's house.
I told Esmeralda all the clues I used
to find her word.

"Great clues!" she said. "But I have trouble. I am now the owner of a possible singing pet."

Suddenly, a turtle crawled in front of us. The turtle was not singing.

"Meet Toots the turtle," Esmeralda said.

"He seems quiet for a singing pet," I said.

"He is very quiet," Esmeralda agreed. "He doesn't growl. Or moo. Or bark. Or even toot. In fact, he doesn't do anything."

"Well, here is something that will sound
good to you, Esmeralda," I said.
"We have your word."
I handed her the muddy pink paper
from Claude's pigpen.
Esmeralda smiled a huge smile.
Then she cried a huge cry.
"'ZooRevue' is not my word!"
"That's because it was *my* word for the
pet concert," Rosamond said. "I thought
Esmeralda could come up with something better."

Sludge and I sadly went on a no-wags
walk to the next house.
Suddenly, Sludge gave a soft bark.
He was sniffing a feather on the sidewalk.
It was a colorful feather.
Maybe it was a parrot's feather.
That gave me an idea.

Chapter Seven
Pip's Parrot

It was time for Sludge and me to go to
Pip's house.
I, Nate the Great, had an idea that Pip's
parrot might be the key to solving this case.
If we found the word at Pip's house,
we would not have to visit Finley's
scary rat or Oliver's slimy eel.

Pip invited us in. His parrot was on a perch.
"Here's the word Rosamond gave me,"
Pip said.
I looked at Pip's word.
The word was "baseball."
The word was wearing a red baseball cap.
It was definitely not Esmeralda's word.
Suddenly, Pip's parrot spoke up.
"I've got it! I've got it!" the parrot shouted.
"SONG-A-PET!"
I smiled at the parrot.

Sludge wagged his tail.
The parrot shouted out again.
"I've got it! I've got it! SONG-A-PET!"
"My parrot has been saying that ever
since we left Rosamond's house yesterday,"
Pip said. "He's driving me crazy."

"Maybe," I said. "But your parrot has also solved the case. He was in the same room as Esmeralda when she was working on her word. Parrots repeat what they hear. Esmeralda told us that she said her word out loud. 'Song-a-pet' is a long word. A strange word. A made-up word. And it is a great name for Rosamond's concert."

"I've got it! I've got it! SONG-A-PET!" said the parrot.

Yes, "song-a-pet" is a great word, I thought. A great word for a terrible concert.

Chapter Eight

Tryout Results

Sludge and I rushed back to
Rosamond's house.
Rosamond and Esmeralda were outside.
"Esmeralda," I called. "Sludge and I found
your word! The word is 'song-a-pet.'"

"Yes!" Esmeralda said. "That's the word I couldn't remember! How did you find it?"

"Pip's parrot told us. He must have heard you say it."

"That makes sense," Esmeralda said. "He was next to me when I came up with it."

"The parrot is a very good detective," Rosamond said.

"Or maybe a very good talker," I said.

"How did the tryouts go?"
I asked Rosamond.
"Not great," she said. "I'm running out
of performers."
"What about all the pets that tried out?"
I asked.
"I choose only the good singers,"
Rosamond said.
"My four Hexes will be an excellent chorus.
I call them the Musical Meows.
But I think the other pets might be jealous
of four cats together.

"Finley's rat makes people scream when they hear him squeal.
So I can't invite him.
Oliver's eel makes a lovely splashing noise when he swims. But splashing isn't singing.
So I can't invite him.
Fang has a big bark, but he drowns out everyone else.
So I can't invite him.
Claude's pig has a nice oink, but Claude might lose her before the concert.
So I can't invite her.
Pip's parrot talks a lot, but he can't sing.
So I can't invite him."
"I, Nate the Great, say that you cannot have a concert," I told her.
Rosamond smiled. "Oh, I know a pet who can sing," she said.
She looked at Sludge.

"Sludge's bark is like a song."

I looked at Sludge.

"Sing," I said.

Sludge did nothing.

Sludge is such a good detective.

He knows when to say nothing.

Chapter Nine

Song-a-Pet!
Song-a-Pet!

I, Nate the Great, and Sludge were home.
"We did not SEE Esmeralda's word," I said.
"We only HEARD it.
We detectives must think about this
over our pancakes and bones."

So we ate and thought.
I, Nate the Great, wondered if
the word had wandered off somewhere.
We had not even seen whether "song-a-pet"
was wearing clothes.
"Hmm . . . clothes," I said.
"Sludge, we wandered too far."
Sludge wagged his tail. He agreed.
We both jumped up.
Sludge rushed to Esmeralda's house.
I followed him.

Esmeralda told us she was wearing
the same sweatshirt she had worn
when her word disappeared.
"Let's dig into the sweatshirt,"
I said to Sludge.
Sludge and I dug into the pocket
of Esmeralda's sweatshirt.

We dug out a pink paper.
"Song-a-pet" was written on it.
It was not wearing any clothes.
It looked fine.
"You solved my case twice!"
Esmeralda yelled.

"You found my lost word
and you found my word on the pink paper.
I want to touch, grab, squeeze, hug,
and kiss all the clues.
I want to kiss *you*."
I held up a hand.

It was time to say good-bye.
Sludge and I took a long walk home.
"I, Nate the Great, say that words
will be fine forever with or without clothes,"
I told Sludge.
"And here are my two favorite words:
'CASE CLOSED'!"

~Extra~
Fun Activities!

What's Inside

Rosamond and Esmeralda were looking for animals that sing. They tried an eel, a pig, a dog, a cat, and a parrot. Nate wondered if their concert would sound better with a different cast. What animals like to sing? This is what he learned.

NATE'S NOTES: Animals That Sing

Mice sing complex songs like birds do. Nate has never heard a mouse sing. That's because their songs are high-pitched. Humans can't hear them.

Frogs sing. Tiny frogs have high voices. Big frogs have deep voices. But the biggest frog in the world doesn't sing at all.

Bats are blind. They use clicking sounds to help them find their way. But male bats also sing. They do it to say: This spot is mine! And they do it to say: Hey, girl bats—let's be friends.

Some types of whales sing.
Nate listened to a recording.
He thought the songs sounded
like a creaky door.

Nate wondered something. What about people? People sing onstage. They sing in cars. They sing in all different styles. Scientists say people sing when they are happy or sad. Singing can make people feel like they belong. It may even make them healthier.

How to Make Your Own Wandering Words

Harry enjoyed cutting words out of sentences. But little pieces of paper can get lost. This is a better way.

Ask an adult to help you.

GET TOGETHER:

- a cookie sheet
- magnetic tape (You can buy it at an office supply store.)
- paper (It can be any color you like.)
- permanent markers
- scissors

8

MAKE YOUR WORDS:

1. Make a list of words you like, similar to the list below. Choose some nouns, some verbs, and some adjectives.
2. Cut pieces of tape about as long as your thumb. Make some a little bigger for long words. Make some a little smaller for short words.
3. Peel the backing off the tape. Stick the paper to the tape.
4. Trim the paper so that it is the same size as the tape.
5. Write a word on each piece. You can also draw shoes, bows, and hats. That way, you can dress up your words like Rosamond did.
6. Move the words around to make new sentences.

NOUNS	VERBS	ADJECTIVES
detective	meow	big
dog	search	muddy
pancake	sing	sharp

9

NATE'S NOTES: Famous Parrots

Esmeralda thought Pip's parrot was good at solving mysteries. Could parrots be detectives? Nate wanted to know. He found a lot of impressive parrots in his search. But none of them solved mysteries.

SNOWBALL the parrot is famous for his dance moves.

POLL was a parrot who belonged to Andrew Jackson. Jackson was the seventh president of the United States. The parrot lived longer than the president did. He even attended Jackson's funeral.

ALEX was an African gray parrot. He belonged to a scientist. She studied his language for 30 years. Alex spoke 100 words. He seemed to understand what the words meant. He was the first animal to ask a question. He wanted to know what color he was. (Gray, of course!)

Funny Pages

Q: What's yellow, weighs one thousand pounds, and sings?
A: *Four thousand canaries.*

Q: What is the most musical part of a fish?
A: *The scales!*

Q: What five-letter word becomes shorter when you add two letters to it?
A: *Short.*

Q: I am an insect. The first part of my name is the name of another insect. What am I?
A: *A beetle.*

Q: What starts with an E and ends with an E and only has one letter in it?
A: *An envelope.*

Q: What is red and smells like blue paint?
A: *Red paint.*

A word about learning with

Nate the Great

The Nate the Great series is good fun and has been entertaining children for over forty years. These books are also valuable learning tools in and out of the classroom.

Nate's world—his home, his friends, his neighborhood—is one that every young person recognizes. Nate introduces beginning readers and those who have graduated to early chapter books to the detective mystery genre, and they respond to Nate's commitment to solving the case and helping his friends.

What's more, as Nate the Great solves his cases, readers learn with him. Nate unravels mysteries by using evidence collection, cogent reasoning, problem-solving, analytical skills, and logic in a way that teaches readers to develop critical-thinking abilities. The stories help children start discussions about how to approach difficult situations and give them tools to resolve them.

When you read a Nate the Great book with a child, or when a child reads a Nate the Great mystery on his or her own, the child is guaranteed a satisfying ending that will have taught him or her important classroom and life skills. We know that you and your children will enjoy reading and learning from Nate the Great's wonderful stories as much as we do.

Find out more at NatetheGreatBooks.com.

Happy reading and learning with Nate!

Solve all the mysteries with

Nate the Great

- ❏ Nate the Great and the Crunchy Christmas
- ❏ Nate the Great Saves the King of Sweden
- ❏ Nate the Great and Me: The Case of the Fleeing Fang
- ❏ Nate the Great and the Monster Mess
- ❏ Nate the Great, San Francisco Detective
- ❏ Nate the Great and the Big Sniff
- ❏ Nate the Great on the Owl Express
- ❏ Nate the Great Talks Turkey
- ❏ Nate the Great and the Hungry Book Club
- ❏ Nate the Great, Where Are You?
- ❏ Nate the Great and the Missing Birthday Snake
- ❏ Nate the Great and the Wandering Word

MARJORIE WEINMAN SHARMAT has written more than 130 books for children and young adults, as well as movie and TV novelizations. Her books have been translated into twenty-four languages. The award-winning Nate the Great series, hailed in *Booklist* as "groundbreaking," has resulted in Nate's real-world appearances in many *New York Times* crossword puzzles, sporting a milk mustache in magazines and posters, residing on more than 28 million boxes of Cheerios, and touring the country in musical theater. Marjorie Weinman Sharmat and her husband, Mitchell Sharmat, have also coauthored many books, including titles in both the Nate the Great and the Olivia Sharp series.

ANDREW SHARMAT is the son of Marjorie Weinman Sharmat and Mitchell Sharmat. *Nate the Great and the Wandering Word* is his second collaboration with his mother.

JODY WHEELER developed a greater-than-average interest in children's books at an early age, having been influenced and encouraged by her great-aunt Opal Wheeler, a prolific writer of books for young readers in the 1950s. Since being trained as a fine artist and educator, Jody has enjoyed working on projects ranging from picture books to educational texts and magazines, and from greeting cards to coloring books. Jody Wheeler divides her time between Manhattan and Balston Spa, New York.